Mine!

by Kevin Luthardt

Granny
229 Campanelli Rd.
Lingenville, WI
54421

Toby and Marcus
2101 Waverly Ln
Horton, IL 60163

Atheneum Books for Young Readers

New York   London   Toronto   Sydney   Singapore

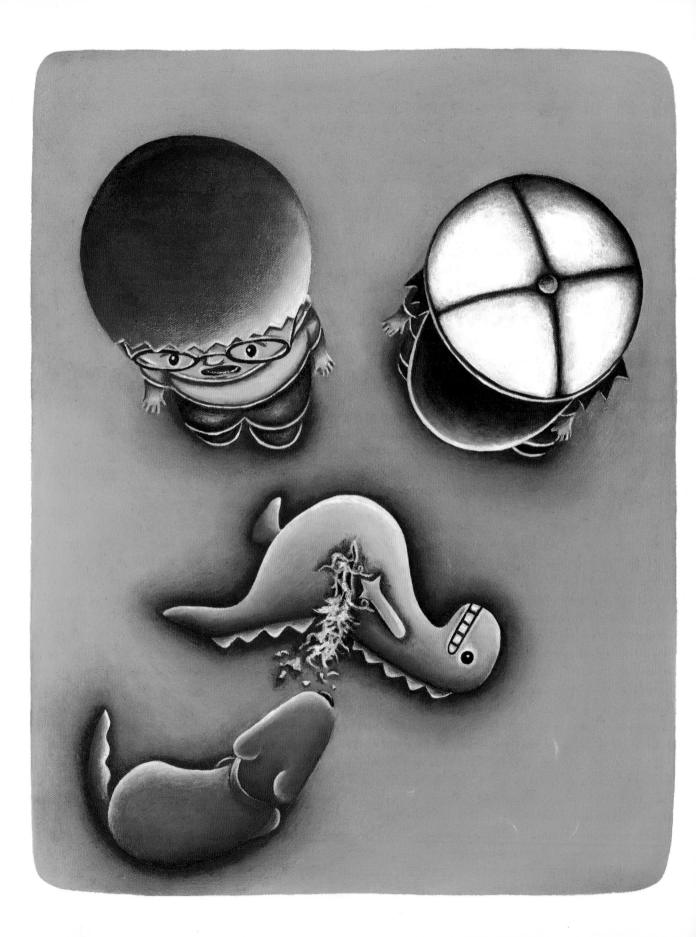

**Thank you Jesus Christ,
my Lord and Savior.**

For Mom and Dad

Atheneum Books for Young Readers   An imprint of Simon & Schuster
Children's Publishing Division 1230 Avenue of the Americas   New York,
New York 10020 Copyright © 2001 by Kevin Luthardt All rights reserved,
including the right of reproduction in whole or in part in any form.   Book
design by Michael Nelson The text of this book is hand-rendered by Kevin
Luthardt. The illustrations are rendered in oil paint. Printed in Hong Kong
2 4 6 8 10 9 7 5 3 1
Library of Congress Cataloging-in-Publication Data: Luthardt, Kevin. Mine!
/ by Kevin Luthardt. p. cm. Summary: Two brothers fight over their new toy
dinosaur until it breaks and they learn to share. ISBN 0-689-83237-0
[1. Brothers—Fiction. 2. Sharing—Fiction. 3. Toys—Fiction. 4. Dinosaurs—
Fiction.] I. Title. PZ7.L9793 Mi 2001 [E]—dc21   99-54317

FIRST
EDITION